D1627478

The Haunting Music

Robina Beckles Willson
Illustrated by Liz Roberts

A & C Black · London

The Comets Series
Series Editor, Amy Gibbs

First published 1987 by A & C Black (Publishers) Ltd.,
35 Bedford Row, London WC1R 4JH.

British Library Cataloguing in Publication Data
Willson, Robina Beckles
   The haunting music.—(The Comets series)
   I. Title   II. Roberts, Liz   III. Series
   823'.914 [J] PZ7

ISBN 0-7136-2879-0

Filmset by August Filmsetting, Haydock, St Helens
Printed in Great Britain by R J Acford Ltd., Chichester.

Mystery in the night

As she walked into Westy House Rebecca thought how odd it was to see her new home for the first time the day that they moved. Her mother propped open the door, and Rebecca walked into a large square kitchen, with rough whitewashed stone walls, and wooden rafters for a ceiling. Her legs felt wobbly, as if she were slightly seasick after the long journey from Liverpool to Somerset.

'Thank goodness we're here before dark,' said her mother. 'Threading through those lanes would have been the last straw. Let's get something to eat. You must all be starving, especially Dad, who's done most of the driving. Then we can all fall into bed. Peter, if you unload the sleeping bags, that will be a step up the wooden hill.'

'But I'm not at all tired,' insisted Rufus, who was only eight and had slept for most of the journey with his hard little head wedged against Rebecca's rigid shoulder.

'Well, the rest of us are,' said his father, 'after all that packing yesterday. And we'll be unpacking it all day tomorrow when the van comes, so we'll need help from everyone.'

After a meal, the family revived enough to look

round the house, so different from the flat they had crammed into at Liverpool.

This house rambled at different levels, up steps from the kitchen to the dining room, a little front parlour and a back room with a huge fireplace for a log fire. Upstairs there were three bedrooms and a bathroom, and above them two attics. But Rebecca made the most exciting find. On the first landing was a locked room.

'Have you a key, do you think, Dad?' she asked.

'Yes, the agent gave me a bunch. There's a padlock. And I've got a titchy key. Let's see if it fits.'

'I wonder what's there, said Peter. 'Gold? Bodies?'

'We'll soon see. This is the right one,' said his father. Matthew Quinn pushed the door open, but they could make out very little. The room was dark, any windows apparently boarded up. 'Get the torch, one of you,' he said. 'It's in my hold-all.'

The torchlight showed heaps of rubble and rubbish all over the floor of a medium sized room. Along the wall opposite their door was a brick fireplace, and another heavy door, bolted.

'Go steady. The floorboards may be rotten,' warned Mr Quinn. He lit his way across the room, followed by Peter, who held the torch while his father slid the bolts back, and shifted another door back as far as it would go. It opened out on to a

stone platform at the top of some wide steps, leading down into the back garden.

'There's some writing, or scribbling on the wall,' said Rebecca.

'Perhaps children,' said her father.

'Another family. How nice,' commented Rebecca.

'I've found something,' said Peter, who had been scrabbling on the sill of a boarded-up window to their left. 'It's a piece of old chain, big hand-made links, look. They must be ten centimetres long. Only seven here. I wish there were more.'

'I'm sure there'll be more, all sorts of junk around,' his father told him. 'That was probably part of a harness. This piece of metal is part of an old buckle. Rooms left like this, derelict and neglected, are bound to have forgotten rubbish. In the old days, they didn't have dustmen collecting. Half the time people just left things or tipped them on heaps. If a room fell out of use, it stayed on as a junk room, with boarded-up windows, getting dirtier every day.'

'It's hard to imagine anyone *not* needing a room,' said Rebecca.

'That's because we've never had enough space. But houses change their uses. Families grow up, and two old people may have lived here, and been glad to bother with less room. And then, when they died, the next owners didn't get round to clearing out the rubbish. Or added their own.'

'I'd like to see exactly what's in here,' said Peter.

'So would I,' added Rebecca.

'We'll settle our stuff in, then you can explore all you wish for the rest of the holidays, as far as I'm concerned. When we bought this house the agent mentioned the old section at the back, saying that we might want to pull it down.'

'You couldn't do that,' protested Rebecca. 'It's part of the house.'

'And might cost a fortune to restore, I suppose, as it's the oldest part, falling to pieces. In fact, he suggested that once it was a little house, then the rest was gradually added on over the years. So the building grew forward! The kitchen is very old too. I think we'll have enough to do for a while, before my new job and your new terms start, without taking on extra rooms.'

Rebecca caught Peter's eye, and knew that he, as she, was quite determined to find out all they could about the ruined room, just as soon as possible, whatever their father said.

★ ★ ★

Although she was extremely tired, when Rebecca went to bed in her sleeping bag on a foam mattress, she could not sleep. It was not only that the floor was hard, and there were no curtains to keep out the last of the daylight. Rufus had been delighted when they all went to bed together. Rebecca wondered if the whole family was sleeping soundly, while she tried to find a comfortable position, and felt the floor moving along, as if they were still driving down the endless motorways. The trees outside her window were not moving, she told herself firmly. She was warm, in her new home, with her precious clarinet beside her, safe in its stiff black case. It was not often that a whole day passed without her playing a note, but they had been travelling so long.

'I'll play tomorrow,' thought Rebecca. 'I hope I'm going to like my new teacher. I'll have to practise hard before my first lesson with him.'

She tried to imagine her new clarinet piece, to

soothe herself to sleep by singing the tune in her head. But the tune went wrong, and another clarinet was playing another tune. Then a different, lower instrument sounded slow deep notes. Violins joined in and played a sort of hymn tune, though not one she could recognise.

Rebecca shifted on the floor, convinced that she was not dreaming, but unable to believe that the music was real. She was sinking into sleep when one of the violins screeched. Startled, Rebecca sat bolt upright in her sleeping bag to listen. She shivered in a night which was growing colder.

Again, the music started. The clarinet led, while violins struggled to keep together and the low instrument boomed.

'I'm *not* asleep and I'm *not* dreaming,' Rebecca told herself, crawling out of her sleeping bag. Then, hugging it round her shoulders like a cloak, she crept outside her room on to the landing.

Everything was utterly still. There was no sound at all except the haunting music, coming, she felt sure, from inside the ruined room. Rebecca was half glad that it was locked up again, because not only was she weary, but also she did not want to face any ghostly players on her own.

2

An exciting find

'I hope you all managed to sleep last night,' said Mrs Quinn the next morning at breakfast. 'I've never known anywhere quieter. I slept like a log.'

'So did I,' said Peter.

'I wasn't tired, so I had a game before I went to sleep,' claimed Rufus.

Rebecca sat sleepily, listening, and realising that no one else had heard the strange music. She felt that if she mentioned it now, everyone would tell her it was only a dream, or tease her for imagining herself playing in an orchestra. So she decided to say nothing until she had seen more of the ruined room, though she was quite glad that Peter wanted to explore it too.

Their opportunity came during the morning while they waited for the removal van to arrive. Rufus was playing outside, so Rebecca and Peter went off together. She told him about the ghostly music: 'And I'm certain I wasn't imagining it, so I'm just a bit scared,' she admitted, as Peter unlocked the padlock.

'Nothing to be scared of in dusty old rubbish,' said Peter. 'But we could let in a bit more light through that door. I want to read the writing on the wall if I can.'

'I don't quite know what I want,' said Rebecca, following him in.

Peter wedged open the door to the garden, and began to read out the scrawls in pencil and crayon on the peeling, greyed whitewash, helped by the torch Rebecca was holding.

'*Hen set on duckling's eggs 18 April 1898*
Hen set on hen eggs 4 May 1898
Planted potatoes March 1886
and a flower drawn, then some dates I can't read.
little bo peep she lost her sheep
Now there's a list of names:
Alice Willie Tilly Lizzy Nellie Mabel Willie Polly.'

'What a family,' said Rebecca. 'Look, there's more by the fireplace, at a slant:
Pigeons hatched Sep 8 1892.'

'That's a long time ago,' said Peter.

'Nothing to do with my music though,' said Rebecca.

'Perhaps you were dreaming after all,' suggested Peter.

'No, I wasn't. And I'm sure there's something hidden here. It's all so old and forgotten.'

'All right. Let's look,' said Peter.

He began to search through the rubble and found a little mug, only about ten centimetres tall. Rubbing it on his shirt sleeve showed that it was rough to the touch and light grey.

'Pewter perhaps,' said Rebecca. 'A child's mug or a measure.'

But she was not diverted by that, or when Peter found several heavy round inkwells made from fawn pot. 'You wouldn't tip those over easily, to make a mess,' he said. 'Perhaps there was a village school here in the old days.'

'It isn't inkwells I'm looking for,' said Rebecca, as he sorted through a pile of old iron nails. They were handmade, heavy and flat, more than eight centimetres long, with stubby, flared-out heads.

'But it's all treasure,' said Peter. 'See, this must have been an old meat hook.'

Rebecca only half listened, picking her way across the rubble to the inner corner of the room, where some repaired brickwork jutted out. As she stepped up close she saw the first turning of a narrow wooden staircase lying behind. The stairs were so old that pieces had splintered and crumbled away from the mended edges. Rebecca glanced back at Peter, absorbed in sorting out the metal collection. She wanted to go up alone. Even though the wood looked soft, almost rotten, with tiny holes, it was quite firm as she walked up carefully, bending and steadying herself with a hand on the treads. Shining her torch into the little room above, she saw a shuttered window and whole sections of the floor decayed beyond repair. But here there was no rubble, only a wooden packing case. Rebecca found that she was holding her breath.

Cautiously she crawled across the broken floorboards and found a large parcel wrapped in a faded blue cloth within the packing case. Feeling sure that it was fragile, Rebecca lifted it out with both hands. She put it on the floor and began to unwind the coverings. First she noticed a musty smell from the cloth, then that the object inside was hard and curved. And it was puzzling.

Rebecca found a large tube of wood, bent into four big curves. The tube had split a little in several places. In parts, the wood was mouldy. Strips of black painted leather and fabric like old bandage were hanging from the body. Stiffening rods of metal were fastened across the curves. It was when

Rebecca saw small holes in the tube, some edged with metal, that she realised that she had uncovered some sort of an instrument.

'Peter,' she called. 'Come and look. I think I've found a musical instrument, but I don't know what it is. Come up the stairs at the corner, but take care. They're rickety.'

'I've found some more writing,' replied Peter.

'This is more exciting than any writing could ever be,' Rebecca told him. 'It must be an instrument. There's a sort of metal tube here bent in a right angle with a mouthpiece, which I suppose joined on to the rest.'

Peter came up beside her. 'It looks like a great snake to me. There's a good length of tube there. It would be harder to blow than a clarinet!'

'The ghost seemed to manage,' said Rebecca, half to herself.

'This is solid enough, not at all ghostly,' said Peter. 'Can we move it downstairs?'

'All right, but it is very old and fragile,' said Rebecca. 'Do you see there are metal bits over some of the holes, like the keys some instruments have. What can it be?'

'Perhaps there'll be a picture in your music dictionary. Or someone will know, like your new music teacher. Wrap it up carefully again, then we can carry it downstairs together. Any other treasures while we're here?'

'Just this bag with some papers in it,' answered Rebecca, showing him a dull orange, envelope-shaped, cloth purse.

'Maybe a clue or two there. We can take some dust off this without it falling to pieces, if we're careful.'

'An instrument as big as this would make a booming sound,' she said as they edged down the stairs, holding it between them, with Peter walking backwards. 'We can take out the papers, but let's keep it in the ruined room for the moment,' suggested Rebecca.

She was already hoping to hear the haunting music again.

3

A new friend and an old instrument

Rebecca did not think that either of her parents would believe in the ghostly music she had heard in the night, and Peter was not really convinced, as he had heard nothing.

But all the family could see for themselves the papers which she took from the cloth purse. They were so brittle that folds had cracked the documents into pieces. The paper was brown, and soft at the edges. The writing was faded, but some could be read.

The first sheet was a list of names. One group was headed: 'The Singers.' At the end of the list was a note saying: 'The instruments are to be kept for sole use of Mellford Choir for time being for ever.'

'Perhaps that was the church choir,' said Mrs Quinn, 'and all those people clubbed together to buy instruments.'

'But why?' asked Rebecca.

'Bands used to play in country churches before the days of organs,' said her father. 'What's this piece? A letter. And look, it's written here. "Mr Thomas Parfitt, Westy House." '

'Our house,' added Mrs Quinn.

'Listen,' said her husband.

' "Mr Parfitt

I am sorry you have waited so long, but I hope for the Best as I think youl find it a full tone and a good pice of work should anything be wanting to it or out or order Mr Hogg will put it to Rights and am your servt.   John Tett.

I am disapointed in sending your Scale and pen to rule lines but will send them next week." '

'It doesn't say what the instrument is,' said Rebecca.

'There's a bill here, set out in the old pounds, shillings and pence, but it's so smudged I can't make it out,' said her father.

'I suppose the pen was a five pronged kind to rule music staves to copy out music,' said Mrs Quinn. 'That would be for copying out parts for the Mellford choir. Can you make out any date on that bill, Rebecca?'

'No, but I think this word is "Clarinette". Rather a nice old spelling,' said Rebecca. 'Though we know that our instrument upstairs isn't a clarinet.'

'Have you tried blowing it?' asked Rufus.

'It's very dusty at the moment, and rather crumbling to pieces. So no, I haven't yet,' answered Rebecca. 'I hardly dare handle it.'

'Probably we should take some advice as we don't know enough,' suggested Mr Quinn.

'Do you think I could mention it to Mr Alexander when we ring him up to fix my lesson?' asked Rebecca. 'It'll be days before we unpack all the books, and I'm longing to know what it really is.'

'His number's on the letter to me about taking you on. No harm in asking,' said her mother.

★ ★ ★

Rebecca felt that her story was slightly tangled when she spoke to Mr Alexander, but he was very friendly, asking her questions in a slow voice with long drawn out vowels.

'It sounds to me like a serpent.'

'Peter said it was like a snake. And is that an instrument?'

'Oh yes. They were big bass instruments, played in church bands, and also carried along in military bands. But a long time ago. I mean over a hundred and fifty years ago, or something like that.'

'It does look old. But not ancient,' Rebecca told him, her voice squeaking with excitement.

'Well, it may have been left there untouched and forgotten. And you say it was well wrapped up?'

'Yes. Would you like to see it?'

'I certainly would.'

'Then come now. We've finished tea,' said Rebecca, taking no notice of her mother's frown and cross look at all the packing cases. 'Then we'll know for sure. It's all right,' she went on, putting down the 'phone. 'He's coming to see the serpent. That's what he thinks the instrument is. Not to see the mess.'

'You can turn to and help clear the mess,' her mother told her. 'There's enough to do without inviting callers almost the first day we're here.'

'I will help, I promise, but he offered. And it isn't every day you find a serpent in your house!'

Rebecca made sure that she was by the door to be able to open it to Mr Alexander. He was a tall young man with a fair beard, and said, smiling, 'So you're Rebecca. I was expecting you to show me your clarinet, not a serpent. What an extraordinarily exciting find.'

'We *think* it's a serpent.'

'From your description, it definitely is.'

Mr Alexander paused in the living room to be introduced to the rest of the family, and to see the papers from the ruined room, while Rebecca hovered impatiently, waiting to take him upstairs.

'We've brought it down here and haven't tried to clean it much yet,' she explained, as soon as they reached the ruined room. 'We'll be keeping this room locked, as the floor isn't very safe, and Rufus might have an accident, if he wandered in here on his own.'

Mr Alexander was kneeling on the dusty floor, inspecting the instrument. 'I had a quick look at a book before I came out, to refresh my memory, and this is a serpent, as I thought.'

'It's such a weird shape for an instrument,' said Rebecca.

'Yes, other instruments have their tubes bent more neatly. And this was hard to make, and fragile, when all the eight feet was snaked in this way.'

'Eight feet!' Rebecca exclaimed.

'Yes, that's why it had to be folded in some way, of course, so that the finger-holes which you spotted could be reached, to blow the deep notes it makes. Even now, it's quite cumbersome to hold for playing. You see there are six finger-holes, and the tube gets gradually wider to the bell at the end.'

'How was it played then?' asked Rebecca.

'This metal crook fitted onto the collar at the thin end of the tube, and the mouthpiece was a bit like a trombone's. You have to puff out with tight lips. It's quite hard for me to get my fingers round it. You need big fingers, and the holes are rather far apart.'

He sat on the low window sill and fixed in the metal crook, then held the serpent downwards, so that its last curl was between his knees. 'I think it's safer to play sitting down, as there's no neck sling to support the weight. And it's quite heavy to hold.'

'It's so huge,' said Rebecca, thinking of her clarinet.

'And may not sound at all,' he warned Rebecca. 'They were made to be airtight, all overlapped, and this may be full of leaks. Also I'm no expert.'

He blew out gently, as if coaxing the old instrument. At first, there was a woofly hoot, and Rebecca tried not to giggle; then a noise a little like a tuba or trombone sounded.

'There. That was rather a peculiar noise, a mixture of brass sound and woodwind, and I suspect nothing like its best. But it isn't quite silent,' said Mr Alexander.

'I was sure it wouldn't be,' said Rebecca. She had liked Mr Alexander as soon as she met him, and now confided in him: 'I knew there was something musical hidden away here, you see.'

'How was that? You've only been in Mellford five minutes, haven't you?' He laughed at her serious face.

'Mr Alexander, do you believe in ghosts?'

He hesitated. 'I do believe we can't account for everything we see.'

'Or hear,' added Rebecca. 'I heard some music coming from this room in the night, and one of the instruments being played was a deep-voiced one, perhaps a serpent, I now think.'

'But it didn't sound all muffled, like the noise I made?'

'Oh no, it was playing under some violins and, I think, clarinets.'

'How strange. That paper downstairs mentioned a clarinet being bought, didn't it?'

'My Dad said perhaps there was a church band playing with the Mellford choir in the old days, before they had an organ in the church.'

'Might have been. I've only lived here a year myself, teaching at the big school in the next village, but I know the church has a little gallery. So it *might* have had a band playing there for the services. You could ask the vicar.'

'But I don't know him.'

'You'll find him very friendly. You didn't know me an hour ago,' said Mr Alexander. 'He might have a lot he could tell you about your Mr Thomas Parfitt, who once lived in Westy House.'

'Could he? How?'

'Churches have a lot of old records, like your letters downstairs, but theirs are registers about births, marriages and deaths, and buying things for the church.'

'You mean, he might know if they bought an organ or a harmonium, and when.'

'Very likely. Go and ask him.'

'I'm supposed to be helping unpack and sort things,' said Rebecca guiltily.

'I don't mean today! You are going to stay here, aren't you?'

'Yes, for ever and ever, I hope. So I can find out all about this serpent and why the music plays in the night and . . .'

'Also find time to play the clarinet, I hope. I've had a good report from your old teacher. So I'm looking forward to hearing you.'

'Oh, I will do some practice before my first lesson,' Rebecca promised.

'All right then. If you get some practice done and just dust this very gently, so that no more comes to pieces, I'll have a word with an antique dealer friend of mine in Bath, to see if he can tell us anything about a serpent turning up out of the blue.'

Rebecca took Mr Alexander back downstairs, and was sorry to see him go off up the lane from Westy House, because she felt she had already made a friend. But his visit had gone so well she was willing to unpack and store endless china in the kitchen, to help wash up supper, then to see that Rufus had his bath and washed behind his ears, and even to play a longwinded game of snakes and ladders with him before she went back to look at the serpent.

4

Detection work

Peter and Rebecca climbed the hill to Mellford church the next morning.

'And did you hear your funny music again last night?' he asked. 'All I heard was an awful squawking cockerel early this morning.'

'I did hear it, and they were playing the same tune. I think it's a carol. I'll have to find out.'

'More detection,' commented Peter. 'I'd always hoped to find treasure, make my fortune, but finding an old instrument seems more like hard work.'

'You needn't come if you don't want to,' Rebecca told him quickly. 'I'll manage.'

'I do have to admit that I'm a bit curious about Thomas Parfitt. He could even be buried here, you realise, though a gravestone as old as that might be impossible to read now. We'll probably have to stick to any parish records the vicar can show us.'

'Then will *you* ask him if we find him at home?'

'Coward. I see I do have my uses,' said Peter. 'To ask your awkward questions for you.'

They walked through the graveyard, where old weathered stones lay in long grass, half covered with Autumn leaves. One stone angel caught Rebecca's eye, but she was guarding the grave of a Susannah Tucker.

'It's very quiet here, isn't it?' she said.

'Only the birds want to go to church this morning,' replied Peter, pushing open a wire-meshed gate into the church porch.

'I'd like to have birds singing in the services,' said Rebecca.

'But no one would like to clear up their droppings,' Peter reminded her. That's why they're kept outside.'

As soon as she went into the church Rebecca looked to the back and saw a little gallery. 'There it is - plenty of room for a band.'

They went past the hanging bell-ropes to a corner staircase, which led to the gallery, overlooking the rest of the church. Rebecca stood in the gallery, and wished she knew more. All that was there were some shabby pews, covered with strips of red carpet, and long wooden kneelers. The walls were bare, and gave no hint of what had been before.

'You could sleep through the boring bits up here,' said Peter.

'A band would have to keep awake, to know when to play,' said Rebecca. 'Let's see what's downstairs.'

They walked down the stone steps, worn into a curve by countless feet, and into the body of the church. On one wall was a list of former vicars, and they saw that the latest was called George Hammond.

'I wish they listed the old choir masters,' said Rebecca. 'Then we might see our Mr Parfitt, and know when he was alive and playing the serpent.'

'Let's have a look at the organ while we're here.'

The organ was locked, with no label or name nearby. They walked slowly through the church, reading out names on memorial tablets, and then strolled in the churchyard, reading names of local families who had lived in Mellford for generations.

'Do we dare just go up to the vicarage, and ask the vicar about our Mr Parfitt?' Rebecca wondered out loud.

'You mean, do I? Of course,' said Peter, 'if you put it like that.'

He went straight up to the vicarage next to the churchyard and rang the door bell. After a long wait an elderly man, with wispy white hair and a smooth smiling face, came to the door.

'Good morning. Can I be of help to you?' he asked.

'Good morning, sir. We've just moved to Mellford and we wondered if you could help us find out more about a Mr Parfitt who once lived in our house.'

'That would be Westy House?'

'You knew him then?' Rebecca blurted, then blushed. 'I mean, you know about Mr Parfitt?'

'There were a lot of Parfitts once in this village. I know that much. And I planned to call on your family when I felt you were a little settled.'

'You knew we were coming then?' asked Peter.

'I try to keep an eye open and say a word of welcome to new-comers. We're quite a friendly community, I think you'll find.'

'We've already met my new clarinet teacher, and he was very nice,' Rebecca told him.

'You're a musician then?'

'I'd like to be. We've found a serpent at Westy House.'

'A serpent! Sounds quite biblical. Remember, in the story of Adam and Eve the serpent who tempted them was told "Upon thy belly thou shalt crawl . . ."'

'She means we found a musical instrument called a serpent,' explained Peter. 'We learnt what it was called from Mr Alexander.'

'You have been busy,' said Mr Hammond vaguely, looking rather puzzled.

Gradually they told him more, and Rebecca finished: 'So we wondered if you could find out when the church bought an organ or a harmonium, and if Thomas Parfitt was a choir master, and if there *was* a church band here once and . . .'

'Just a minute, young lady,' he interrupted her gently. 'That will have to be enough for the moment. I'll check through the parish records, and see what I can find, but it will take time. And that is what I am always short of, as I have to take care of more than one parish. The problem is that there is so much to attend to today, looking after all my people as well as this old building, that I have little time to study the past, even though I live among so many relics. But,' he looked more cheerful, 'when I retire, I shall enjoy writing a little history of this village.'

'Is that soon?' asked Rebecca, and blushed again. 'I'm sorry. That sounded rude.'

'I know I look ancient, but it won't be quite yet. Mind you, as I get older, the present and the past do seem closer together.'

'Do you mean the past can come back?' Rebecca asked. 'Does it sort of live on, do you think?'

'She's got ghosts on the brain because we've moved into such an old house,' Peter commented.

'We do get reverberations from the past in old buildings, I feel,' said the vicar. 'And, after all, if you believe in a life of the spirit, as I do, why not spirits returning?'

'There are more than reverberations at Westy House,' Rebecca told him. 'I'm sure I heard music in the night, before I found the serpent.'

'No one else but you?'

'No one else so far.'

'I suppose we have to leave some things unexplained,' suggested Mr Hammond.

'I can't leave it. There must be a reason why I was led to the serpent. I'm treating it as a mystery to be solved,' Rebecca declared.

'And dragging me in to help,' added Peter.

'Then I'll do all I can for you,' said Mr Hammond. 'It is strange, I confess, that the music only sounds for you, Rebecca.'

* * *

On the way home Peter said he was hungry, so they called at the village shop and waited to be served.

Rebecca listened to the 'Yaas' as people nodded agreement in lengthy conversations. Although the small shop was also crammed with goods it could not have been more unlike the supermarket they had often used in Liverpool. And their old corner shop there did not sell groceries, video films, stationery, clothes, sweets, greengroceries, newspapers, meat, household goods and toys all jumbled together. The talking went over Rebecca's head as she stared round. She had to concentrate to understand exactly what was said, as some of the Somerset accents gave English a different sound as they sang up and down in rambling sentences.

Peter had been choosing from crisps stacked in their boxes, and went up to the shopkeeper, who, it seemed, was called Evalina.

'You're visitors here then, are you?' she asked him.

'We've just moved from Liverpool.'

'A bit different down here. You like the village life do you?'

'Yes, I think we do.'

'And this is your sister?'

'I'm Rebecca, and we've moved to Westy House.'

'Have you now? That's a fine old house.'

'It is,' Rebecca agreed. 'Do you know it?'

'I've seen it all my life, since a child,' said Evalina.

'Did you ever know of a family called Parfitt living there?' asked Rebecca, slightly shy of the other people in the shop, looking for goods, but listening in at the same time.

'I can't say I did,' said Evalina. 'Granfer, would you recollect the name Parfitt in the village?'

'The last of the Parfitts died when I was a boy.

Lost in the Great War,' replied an old man who was sorting through a crate of potatoes and putting the big ones into a plastic bag.

'And did they live at our house?' asked Rebecca.

'The old lady, his mother, was down there when he went missing. Within days she died, of a broken heart.' Granfer plonked his potatoes on to the scale, and there seemed no more to be said.

'Sorry we can't help you,' said Evalina, smiling at them. 'I hope you're going to be very happy in Mellford. I think we're quite a friendly lot round here.'

On the way home Peter said, 'They are friendly here, aren't they? Don't seem to mind us coming. Perhaps they'll sort of include us in the village.'

'Hope so. Everyone I pass says hello to me.'

'Oh they're just humouring you, having heard already what a nutcase you are about music,' Peter told her.

★　★　★

When they reached home Peter and Rebecca were set to work sorting out their bedrooms. Rufus was meant to be helping too, but hovered between the boys' attic rooms and Rebecca's room, where she kept dipping into books rather than arranging them on shelves. She looked up SERPENT and found that Mendelssohn, Wagner and Verdi had all written for the instrument. There was nothing in her book about church bands.

Then she played a few scales on her clarinet, which only reminded her of the serpent lying in the ruined room. So, making sure that her mother was still busy in the kitchen and not coming to check her efforts, she went again to look at the serpent. She felt drawn back to hold and feel it for herself, noticing this time the little cupped mouthpiece of yellowing ivory.

Rebecca put her mouth to it and blew out in a 'raspberry', but no sound came. 'I haven't the knack or the puff to do anything with it,' she thought. 'I don't expect anyone of my size and age could be a serpentist and play this big instrument. But that won't stop me doing something about the serpent now I've found it.'

5

A silent serpent

Although all the family by now had seen the serpent, Rebecca insisted on keeping it in the ruined room, so that each night she would hear her music. One night, she left her bedroom and went over to the door, but didn't dare go in, in case somehow she broke a spell. Peter offered to go in with her, but, as he did not hear any music, he did not have the same mixed feelings of pleasure and fear. Not that the music was beautiful. Sometimes the violins were out of time with the steady booming beat of the serpent. Sometimes the clarinets squealed and played out of tune.

'It's as if they are practising their carol for ever,' Rebecca thought to herself. 'I wonder if that means they used to practise here in Westy House? As the serpent is here, I suppose it belonged to Thomas Parfitt, and he put it away upstairs. Or it was wrapped up when he died. Perhaps the band went on playing here when the organ took their place in church. If I opened the door when I heard the music, would he be sitting there playing his serpent?'

The telephone rang and she was called to speak to Mr Alexander.

'Rebecca, I've contacted my dealer friend. Would you like to visit Bath with me, to show him your serpent?'

Rebecca hesitated for a moment, not wanting to move the serpent.

'He'll be able to tell us how it could be restored, or if it could be made to play the proper sound. Would you like that?'

'Yes, I think I would,' she answered rather doubtfully.

'We can take good care of it, and wrap it up so it won't come to any harm in my car,' he told her.

Rebecca couldn't admit that she was worried about losing her haunting music, as that sounded superstitious, and moving the serpent was one way of finding out more. It could be put back that night. 'Or would I dare to keep it in my room?' she asked herself. 'It is only a wooden instrument, after all.'

'Is that all right then?' Mr Alexander asked. 'You'd better check with your mother.'

Mrs Quinn was intrigued. 'It might be valuable. And must be very old. Perhaps he'll be able to date it for you.'

'I hope he might be able to make it play better,' said Rebecca.

She set off with Mr Alexander with the serpent wrapped in an old blanket and stored in its wooden crate. The antique dealer's shop was in a side street near Bath Abbey, and he took them at once into a back work room, where the serpent was un-wrapped.

'So what do you think of it, Malcolm?' asked Mr Alexander.

'Quite a find,' answered the dealer, looking over the instrument with the utmost care. 'I love the way they painted the inside of the bell red. It seemed a tradition to do that, and to paint the leather black. You needed huge hands to reach these holes, didn't you? And I think you also needed a strap or cord like a modern saxophone sling to support it.'

'I tried it out sitting down,' Mr Alexander told him, 'and got a bit of a note.'

'Good going, as there are quite a few cracks in the glueing of the joints. It's an English one, I'm sure of that, not a military model.'

'We think it was played in church,' Rebecca added, explaining about the documents they had found.

'Yes, I'm sure you're right. I think we would date it at about 1815.'

'Amazing really that it's survived at all.'

'From your story, it was just stowed away and forgotten,' said Malcolm. 'And remember, serpents did go right out of fashion. Modern brass instruments with valves, less tricky to play and look after, took their place.'

'We hope to find out, but we think a harmonium

or a church organ took its place at Mellford,' said Rebecca. 'I'm sure Mr Parfitt must have been sad when his band was no longer needed.'

'Very likely. So now this is an antique to cherish, as there's only one person I know who makes new serpents today.'

'But I look at it as an instrument to be played, even if I couldn't manage myself till my hands are bigger,' said Rebecca.

'Now there is the problem. Either it can be patched up to look handsome, to hang on your wall. Or it can be restored to a new working life.'

'Restored, of course,' said Rebecca quickly.

'Then you had better start saving now,' said Malcolm, smiling at her. 'You see, it's not the sort of thing I could do myself. A specialist would have to take it to pieces, mend any holes, glue it together, bind it with cloth, then leather, paint it all, then fix the metal parts on again: many hours of painstaking work, so a great deal of money.'

'How much is a great deal?' asked Rebecca.

'I rang up the only man I know who restores serpents, and he said everything would depend on its condition. Old serpents fetch between £600 and £1200 in sales. Restoring could cost from £50 upwards, but perhaps well over a hundred.'

'We'd never afford that,' said Rebecca. 'I had to save up to pay towards my clarinet.'

'Well put it like this,' suggested Malcolm

kindly. 'You could sell it . . .'

'Certainly not,' Rebecca interrupted.

'Or you could clean it up yourself gently, with a little leather soap, and a lot of care. Then one day, you might be in a position to restore it to full working order for yourself.'

'I think my Dad would have to win the pools or something.'

'You never know what might happen,' said Mr Alexander. 'After all, finding the serpent was a complete surprise, a piece of good luck.'

'Yes,' Rebecca agreed, though she privately added to herself that she knew there was going to be something there as witness to her haunting music.

They talked more, and Mr Alexander thanked Malcolm for all his help and advice, while Rebecca wrapped up the serpent, feeling numb.

On the way home, Mr Alexander said, 'Had you hoped it would be an easier job then, cost less?'

'I hadn't really hoped anything,' Rebecca replied, 'except doing something with the serpent, to show we've found it.'

'A sort of celebration. We'll have to think,' he said. 'Keep up your clarinet for now. I'm pleased with what you've done so far. I think if you're prepared to work hard, you could be very good, if that encourages you.'

'A bit,' Rebecca admitted.

'And you could add being a serpentist later on. How's that?'

★ ★ ★

Nobody at home was surprised by Rebecca's account of her visit to Bath, and she realised that only she was disappointed that somehow the miracle of finding the serpent could not continue.

'You'll have to make something of it all,' said her mother. 'It'll come.'

'But the only thing for instruments is playing,' Rebecca maintained obstinately.

'There's more to music than just playing, now isn't there? Still, if you go and play your clarinet, that will cheer you up.'

But although Rebecca did a long practice, working through all her scales and arpeggios before she started her new pieces for Mr Alexander, she was restless, with the serpent still in her mind. It was only tantalising to look at the serpent again, so she decided to walk up to the church, and revisit the gallery, where perhaps it had once been played in services.

She met Mr Hammond in the church yard, and he said, 'Just the person I wanted to see. I've found out something that will interest you. In an old Churchwarden's Account Book, I came across an entry which mentioned buying a new clarinet for the church band in 1817. And in that year a Mr Thomas Parfitt of Westy House was married.'

'So there *was* a band here, and he was alive then and perhaps playing our serpent in the band.'

'But not at his own wedding, I trust.'

'That does make it seem more real,' said Rebecca rather wistfully. 'I did want to bring it to life in some way, you see. And we definitely can't afford to have it restored properly.'

'No, that will have to be a hope for the future,' Mr Hammond agreed. 'But bringing things to life can be done in different ways. You think about it. There will be a purpose. Now I must get on, though I'd rather gossip with you than take the meeting I have to attend.'

He turned to go into the vicarage, then called back, 'And I found out one thing more. The church bought a harmonium in 1842.'

'Thank you,' Rebecca called back. 'That means we know the band probably lasted till then. I'll tell Peter. He likes working out the history part of it.'

'And good luck to you with the rest,' said Mr Hammond.

Thinking about the serpent and the band, she

looked in at the church, but it was silent and still; no life there. Rebecca walked down the hill back home, wondering what she could do now. She went to Evalina's to buy some chocolate, and found the shop unusually quiet, with Evalina unpacking goods.

'It seems early for Christmas stock, but it gets earlier every year, seems to me,' she said. 'I run a Christmas club, you know.'

'What's that,' asked Rebecca.

'People pay in so much every week, like saving, then they've some money put by for their Christmas shopping.'

'Sounds a good idea. I'll tell my Mum,' said Rebecca. 'Is it fun here in the village at Christmas?'

'Not as good as when I was young, as we all say,' answered Evalina. 'But I do like the old fashioned Christmas myself, the family gatherings, decorated trees, carols and all that.'

'I like carol singing,' said Rebecca.

'Then you're welcome to come carolling at our door,' Evalina told her. 'I can't bring to mind how long ago it was that we had proper carolling round the village.'

'How long ago,' Rebecca kept repeating the words to herself on the way home, sucking pieces of chocolate to make it last. By the time she reached Westy House she had an idea.

6

Rebecca's idea for the village

'What I'd like to do, you see, is to make a new village band. Bring to life the old Parfitt band, in a way,' Rebecca explained. 'But I suppose you think that mad. And impossible, when we've only lived in the village for a few weeks.'

'Not mad, or no madder than usual,' said Peter. 'And not impossible either.'

'You mean you'd help me?' Rebecca asked eagerly.

'Well, I can't play an instrument. One in the family making all that hooting and screeching is plenty,' Peter answered.

'But you *can* sing in tune.'

'So?'

'So we could have a band and try and get it going in time for Christmas carols round the village.'

'Do you think people in the village would like that?' asked Peter doubtfully.

'I know one who would. Evalina said nobody had gone round doing proper carolling for years and years. So we wouldn't have any rivals.'

'And we could collect for a good cause, not just ourselves, or the mend-the-serpent fund,' Peter went on. 'But we haven't a big enough family, with a Willie, Lizzy and Tilly and all the other little Parfitts I tracked down in Mr Hammond's Register of Christenings.'

'I've told you, it would be a *village* band.'

'We'd need some singers, and some players then. How do we find those?'

'Dad sings, not only in the bath. He'd know the old carols. Rufus is sure to want to join in. And he might rope in some of his friends in the school recorder club.'

'Who'll all play out of time and out of tune,' added Peter.

'We'll never get a band together if we start fussing with auditions, expecting only marvellous players. I'll just make sure the players can read music and hope for the best. Now, who else?'

'We could ask Mr Hammond if any of his church choir would help. It's only a small choir, but someone might.'

'And we could ask Evalina what she thinks. Her shop is the centre of village gossip, after all. Let's go and ask her straight away.'

Evalina was enthusiastic. 'I'll tell people myself, but you could put a notice in the window, if you like. It's only ten pence a week. And that might bring in an offer or two.'

'If we get all the village playing and singing, there'll be no one to cough up money,' said Peter.

'I'll be at home for you,' promised Evalina. 'I never was much of a singer. I just like to hear the carols. And, if you give me warning, I expect there'll be something waiting here for you.'

'Of course. That's the good bit. Being asked in for refreshments, for our dry throats,' said Peter. 'Mum would lay on food too I should think.'

'If you have several calls for a bite, you can manage quite a lot in one evening,' Evalina told them.

Peter and Rebecca went into a corner of the shop and composed an advertisement on the card Evalina provided. After a lot of discussion and many rough copies they gave her:

COME AND JOIN THE NEW
MELLFORD BAND.
ALL SINGERS AND PLAYERS WELCOME.
FIRST OUTING, CHRISTMAS CAROLS
ROUND THE VILLAGE.
PLEASE 'PHONE PETER OR REBECCA
FOR DETAILS: MELLFORD 3779.

They paid ten pence, bought some crisps and wandered home feeling slightly dazed by their own cheek.

So when the telephone rang that evening neither Peter nor Rebecca went to answer, and Rufus took the call.

'It's for you, Rebecca.'

'What shall I say?' she asked Peter. 'We haven't worked out much.'

'Take the name and 'phone number and say we'll be in touch later. We're raising talent now.'

'Come ON,' said Rufus. 'It's Mr Alexander for you, Rebecca.'

'Oh!' exclaimed Rebecca, hurrying to the 'phone. 'I'm sorry. We put an advertisement in the shop, and I thought someone might be ringing about that.'

'You're not selling the serpent?'

'Never,' said Rebecca. 'No, I had an idea, really coming from the serpent and talking to everybody about it.' She explained the plan for a village band, and Mr Alexander listened well. Then he said, 'Do you need my help, or do you want to conduct it yourself?'

'Me conduct! I wouldn't dare. I never thought of that,' exclaimed Rebecca. 'Anyhow, I want to play the clarinet, like in the haunting music.'

'Then would you like me to give them a beat? It does keep people together.'

'We'd love that,' answered Rebecca. 'Peter's going to sing; I'm sure he wouldn't want to conduct.'

'I wouldn't.'

'But it would bring a scratch band together if a

real musician led them and told them what to do.'

'I won't be too demanding,' promised Mr Alexander, 'as they'll be doing it for fun, after all. Let me know how the recruiting goes, and we'll fix a meeting. There'll be a lot to decide. Which carols, which good cause and how we practise the band.'

'My idea is more complicated than I realised,' admitted Rebecca. 'I think we're taking on a lot.'

'Why not? The village hasn't had anything like this at Christmas for years. Much better than sitting gaping at television all the time.'

'If we get any offers I'll be pleased to make a start,' said Rebecca.

★   ★   ★

'You'll get millions of recorders,' stated Rufus.

'I haven't got one yet,' said Rebecca.

'All my class learns,' said Rufus. 'We're made to.'

'I was hoping for some of the keen good players in your recorder club,' Rebecca told him. 'Nobody's rung yet.'

'They won't *offer*, said Rufus scornfully. 'You'll have to ask them.'

'Even at your age you don't think they'll volunteer?' asked Rebecca. 'Oh dear. But you'll help, won't you?'

'Oh yes. I know what I want to play.'

'The recorder,' said Rebecca.

'No. I want to play the drum. The scouts have

one, and they said I could borrow it if I was careful.'

'But Rufus, you can't play the drum.'

'I can learn. I always played it in our percussion band. I have an excellent sense of rhythm.'

'Oh have you. And who told you that?'

'The teacher at our old school. Anyhow, you said any offer would be accepted, and it would be a scratch band, as you call it. So you can't turn me down just because I'm your brother.'

Rebecca had to agree, though she was beginning to wonder what noise a mixed set of unskilled players would produce. 'All right, you borrow the drum and we'll work out a part for you when we've chosen the carols.'

'I shall be putting in a lot of practice,' Rufus told her with dignity.

★   ★   ★

Gradually offers trickled in. A girl of nine who lived nearby came and showed Rebecca her three-quarter sized violin.

'I think I could play the tune of any well-known carol,' she offered. 'My teacher said she'd hear me in my lessons if I had the music.'

'That would be lovely,' said Rebecca. 'We'll let you know about the first run-through, and we'll certainly give you your part to learn. My clarinet teacher's working them out.'

'Do you want to hear me play?' asked Anne.

'No, I mean, yes please,' said Rebecca, catching a disappointed expression. 'My teacher, Mr Alexander, will conduct us, or bring us together.'

'How marvellous,' said Anne. 'I've never played in an orchestra.'

'I think,' Rebecca told her, 'that this will be more of a band.'

Then she heard Anne play a short piece, and was pleased that there was none of the whining and grinding of some of the players at her old school.

'So you're our first string player,' said Rebecca, thanking her and noting her full name and address.

★   ★   ★

An old man stopped Rebecca in the street and

asked, 'Are you the young lady who's starting up a village band? Our Evalina was telling me.'

'Yes, me and my brother. And my clarinet teacher,' answered Rebecca.

'Then could you make use of an accordian player? I only play for my own pleasure, but I can hold a tune.'

'Can you read music too?' Rebecca asked rather shyly, not wanting to sound unwelcoming.

'A bit, but I've still got my good ear, and I reckon I could join in any of the old favourites, if it's carols you'll be playing. I pick up tunes fast, still play at parties.'

'We're thinking of carols, round the village.'

'Just like when I was a boy. Always cold and always hungry, looking forward to the next port of call.'

'So you remember it happening here?' Rebecca asked eagerly. 'Then you could give us any tips.'

'Dress up warm, and make sure of some kind folk to have you indoors,' said the old man.

'Evalina has offered, and my Mum will give us something too, at Westy House. I think Mr Hammond might as well.'

'Then that's three, well spaced down the village. Give me a sit-down too.'

Rebecca would have loved to ask how old he was, as he looked as if he were in his eighties, but she just took his name, Jecoliah Button, and promised to call and tell him about the first band rehearsal.

Three singers from the church choir offered to sing, and the organist said he would sing or play the flute, whichever would help most. A boy at Peter's school, who lived at Mellford, offered to play the trumpet, and from Rufus's school three recorder players signed on.

'I think we're getting enough people, though goodness knows what they'll all sound like together,' said Rebecca.

'Murder, I should imagine,' said Peter. 'We'll have to bellow loudly to drown them. What carols are we going to sing, by the way?'

'I must start looking today,' said Rebecca. 'Then I can talk to Mr Alexander about copies and parts and all that.'

'It's quite a business,' commented Peter.

'But it's what I want to do,' said Rebecca.

★   ★   ★

That night she stayed awake deliberately, waiting to hear the haunting music. When the violin squeaked she thought of Anne, and when the serpent sang its loud notes she wondered who could supply such a satisfying bass part. But what she was really trying to do was to memorise the familiar tune they played so often, so that she could try and track it down in a book of carols lent to her by Mr Alexander.

'I wish,' thought Rebecca, 'I could write it down as I hear it, like a real musician. But I *think* I've got it in my head.'

When the music faded away she took out her clarinet and began to play the first line of each carol in the collection, trusting that the haunting one would not slip out of her mind. It was very late, and she hoped no one would wake up. 'They don't hear my other music, but they might hear this,' she thought, trying out *As I sat on a sunny bank.*

'And I must keep awake, or I'll forget the tune again by morning,' Rebecca told herself, turning to number eight. She played the first line, then played on, shivering with delight. It was the carol of the ghostly players, she was certain: *Come all you worthy gentlemen, That may be standing by.*

'Fancy finding it so quickly,' she thought. 'That *must* be our first choice, their Somerset carol,' Rebecca decided, looking at the last verse.

God bless our generation
Who live both far and near,
And we wish them a happy, a happy New Year!
'I can't wait to show Mr Alexander.'

* * *

'There is a Somerset wassail with the chorus,
No harm, boys, harm; no harm, boys, harm;
And a drop or two of cider will do us no harm.'
Mr Alexander told Rebecca. 'But I think the north country one is better for us:

49

Here we come a-wassailing
Among the leaves so green.'

'Yes, because that's the well-known tune,'
Rebecca agreed. 'Less to learn, and I like the begging verse,

We have got a little purse
Of stretching leather skin;
And we want a little of your money
To line it well within.'

'You see the verses are meant to be solos,' he
went on. 'What I suggest is that you play those on
the clarinet, and we'll persuade some singers to
sing solos, then the band can join in the 'Love and
joy' choruses. I'll write out some band parts, and I
can photo-copy them on the Post Office machine.
Your dad sings bass, I gather? If he can hold that
part it would be fine, but most of the singers will
pick up the tune by ear and follow as they can.'

'We haven't got a low instrument yet to take the
place of a serpent, have we? In the Somerset carol
I've been hearing it sounds so strong, it sort of
holds the others up.'

'I know what you mean. I'll be trying to hold
them together, but we could do with a bassoon. Or
a bass clarinet would do. Perhaps I could enlist
another pupil. I'll think about that.'

'I can't think of anything else much but the
carols,' Rebecca admitted. 'I do hope everyone
turns up for the first rehearsal.'

7

Rehearsing and quarrelling

'I hope,' said Mr Alexander, 'that you've all found time to look at your parts.'

Anne nodded vigorously, with her violin bow clenched tightly, and her cheeks bright pink with excitement. Other members of the band smiled vaguely in a way Rebecca recognized. People looked like that at school when they hadn't learned things by heart, and hoped they wouldn't be asked to recite.

'There's only one way of finding out,' added Mr Alexander. 'And that's to have a run through. The Wassail song is one most of you will have sung or played before. It's a good dancing rhythm, so we'll have Rufus beating it out, tum-te tum, tum-te-tum, to keep us going, even if we're standing still! All the verses will be solos. Any volunteers?'

Three from the church choir offered to sing, and Mr Alexander persuaded two of the recorder players to sing, as a duet:

We are not daily beggars
That beg from door to door,
But we are neighbours' children
Whom you have seen before:

'Rebecca will give you the notes, playing with

you, and Rufus the beat. So you'll be fine,' he told them.

When everybody joined together in the chorus Rebecca thought it a terrible din. She looked up at the gallery, wondering if Mr Parfitt's players ever made such a noise. But Mr Alexander was not at all dismayed.

'Not bad for a first try,' he commented. 'Now I wonder how many of you could hear at all what your neighbour was playing? If you could only hear yourself, you were playing too loudly. Playing in a band is about listening to other people too. *And* watching me. Then we might be a little less all over the place. Let's have the singers first, just with Rebecca and Rufus.'

Rufus beat away doggedly, looking hot and bothered, but Mr Alexander just gave him a quick glance.

The singers sang through the chorus, and were urged to smile. 'You're singing "God bless you", so it had better come out warm and friendly in tone. Now the instruments, please. Crisp rhythm will make it clear. Listen to my friend on the bass clarinet. He's your foundation. Neat chords, not spread on the accordion, please, so we're all together.'

Mr Button nodded where he was sitting on the front row. The other players were standing to one side of Mr Alexander, and the singers in a group. Rebecca marvelled at his patience when players came in late and then managed to play wrong notes, but he encouraged and teased them through *While Shepherds watched their flocks by night*: 'Polite words only, please, not to shock the village! And then *O little Town of Bethlehem*. This is a favourite of mine, so, if you play and sing it well, I might even come on the night!'

After that rehearsal Mrs Quinn made them hot coffee or orange squash, then whisked a protesting Rufus home to bed. Rebecca stayed to talk to Mr Alexander while Peter tried to get a note on the trumpet.

'It was a start,' said Mr Alexander, suddenly looking tired and sitting down, holding a mug of coffee between his hands. 'A way to go, but we'll get there, so people won't mistake us for a party brawl outside their doors on Christmas Eve.'

'We've only fixed one more rehearsal. Is that enough then?' asked Rebecca.

'Yes, because I think that those who hadn't looked at their parts will have a little try-over at home: and those who have learned already will be keen to practise to play better. Like that brave little Anne, all alone on the fiddle.'

'I'm more worried about Rufus. He can't really keep time. It's hard for him, but he's too cocky to admit that, having borrowed the drum.'

'He'll cope if he has a bit of help on the side. Just some coaching really. Do you think you could do that, Rebecca?'

'I don't know if he'd listen to me,' Rebecca answered doubtfully.

'No. He must learn to listen to himself, to know what he's playing! But it would help to have his part sorted out on his own.'

'I'll try then,' said Rebecca, realising how much time Mr Alexander was giving to the village band she had started. 'I could never have made them perform like you did tonight,' she went on. 'My idea wouldn't have got going at all without you.'

'It is my job, don't forget,' said Mr Alexander, yawning. 'You played well tonight, and I did see you glance at me from time to time too!'

'I'll know the carols by heart for the day, I hope,' said Rebecca. 'Then I won't need to look at the music.'

'There will be a bit of light, but no one to hold up the music for you, so do learn them. That reminds me. Torches, lanterns. Peter, we must work those out. Could you rustle some up? Did I tell you that I got the permit from the police to do house-to-house collecting with carol singing? And the village bobby said he hadn't been asked for one for donkey's years.'

While he was talking to Peter, Rebecca looked up at the gallery, and thought she saw shadowy people moving about. Without explaining anything, she hurried to the back of the gallery. Her heart was thumping with excitement. But no one was there.

It did not stop Rebecca feeling that ghostly players had been listening to the rehearsal. 'I hope you were pleased with what I've managed so far to bring back a band to Mellford,' she whispered to the empty air.

★   ★   ★

On Saturday morning, Rebecca started to coach Rufus, full of good intentions. But somehow it didn't work. He didn't want to go through all his carols, and was longing to go out and play football with another boy.

'Mr Alexander didn't say anything,' he grumbled.

'He just asked me to go through them with you, to practise the rhythms a bit, so you're sure of them, as he hasn't time to go through everyone's part separately. That would take all night, with our mixed band.'

'I know my part,' said Rufus obstinately.

'But not every note perfect. I want it to be so good, my serpent band,' said Rebecca, half to herself.

'It's not your band. It's the village band,' argued Rufus. 'And you said anyone could join in if they could read their tunes. So it's not fair picking on me, just because I'm your brother.'

'I know it's the village band. That's the idea.

But we can't have you banging away out of time.'

'I don't bang,' shouted Rufus. 'I beat. You're just bossing me around as if you owned the band and the village, and Westy House and everything in it. And I'm going to play football.'

But as he spoke the 'phone went, and he was told that his friend would not be coming, as he had a tummy bug. 'Lucky him,' commented Rufus. 'He's not pushed around by *his* sister. And now I'm caught indoors, I suppose.'

'You can go out when you like,' said Rebecca, feeling tempted to break the drum over his head. 'It's just that I promised Mr Alexander we'd go through the carols.'

'You can go through your own part and stop squeaking on the high notes, *if* you can,' said Rufus, rushing out of the room and slamming the door.

'What on earth is going on?' asked Mrs Quinn. 'Early Christmas spirit breaking out?'

'Rufus is in a temper because I wanted him to practise his part with me, as he hasn't got all the rhythms perfect yet.'

'I should think not,' said Mrs Quinn. 'He is only eight.'

'But he wanted to do it.'

'Of course he did, and he's been struggling ever since. He *has* been practising in the kichen, when you've been in your bedroom, or in the ruined room cleaning the serpent. And last night, when I got him home, he was so worn out with the rehearsal, your Dad had to carry him up to bed. So take it easy.'

'It's just that I want it to be so good,' Rebecca tried to explain. 'Not for me, but for the serpent, for finding the music here. It sounds silly . . .'

'Not silly, but you have to remember that is *your* dream, if you like. Other people can only do their best. You'll find they'll come out better on the night, with extra excitement. But note perfect playing doesn't come from bands who are just volunteers helping to celebrate Christmas, and collect for a good cause.'

'Perfect playing I suppose is a dream,' said Rebecca slowly, suddenly remembering that her haunting music was of a band practising, not always playing together or in tune.

'Try again later,' her mother suggested. 'Play your clarinet with him. And be as tactful as you can.'

The day did not improve. It began to pour with rain, and Rebecca was stuck with some homework. Peter had retreated to his bedroom, saying he must not be disturbed, as he had to finish a project before the end of term. Mrs Quinn told Rebecca to wait and ask her father for help when he came in from shopping at the do-it-yourself warehouse. So Rebecca hung about the house, not wanting to settle to anything, so ruffled by Rufus that she did not even want to play the clarinet.

She guessed he was sulking somewhere, and to make sure of not running into him she went to the ruined room to look at the serpent. But this time there was a blank.

On the floor the crate was empty. Rebecca felt

quite dizzy as thoughts flashed through her mind.
Where was the serpent? She hadn't moved it. Who
could have taken it? Why was it not in its place,
wrapped up as she left it? Where *was* the serpent?

She shone her torch all round the room, sick
with disbelief. She stumbled across to the old staircase and hurried to the upper room, not caring
about the rickety floorboards. But the serpent was
nowhere there.

Rebecca felt as if she were in a nightmare, the
kind where she wanted to scream and no sound
would come out. She rushed back into the house
and down to the kitchen gabbling and nearly
crying as she told her mother:

'My serpent's gone. It's disappeared.'

'Not more trouble. Now calm down,' said her
mother. 'It can't have done. You've moved it and
forgotten, that's all.'

'Anything could happen in that room,' said
Rebecca wildly.

'Don't be ridiculous. It was locked with a padlock. You've just been doing too much. You're all

eyes. Too little sleep and too much music and . . .'

'Never too much music,' interrupted Rebecca.

'We'll think. Has Peter moved it?'

'Of course not. He wouldn't do anything to it without me. And we've kept it in there because of the music.'

'I think it's high time the serpent came out of the ruined room, and we had it hanging on the wall, in your room if you like, until we can afford to have it restored. You're getting far too worked up about it in there.'

'But what if the music stopped?'

'Probably the music will stop one day. You are having your own band, you see,' said Mrs Quinn.

'But I *need* the serpent now. It's the point of beginning the band in the first place,' Rebecca wailed. 'Even if I can't play it. You don't understand. Where *can* it have gone?'

'Solid wooden instruments don't vanish into thin air. Now. When did you see it last?'

'It was there before the rehearsal. I went and looked. Then I went straight to bed when Peter and I came home.'

'Can you remember if you got up in the night to listen to the music?'

'How did you know?'

'Never mind. I sleep lightly. But I do think we'll have it out of that room when we find it.'

'If we find it.'

'Of course we will,' Mrs Quinn assured her, though she looked relieved when she saw her husband drive up to the back door. He came dripping into the kitchen, drenched even in the short time outside the car shopping. So it was some minutes before they could tell him about the missing serpent.

Rebecca brooded all through lunch. Rufus was speechless, sulking, and Peter was still thinking about his project. So Mr and Mrs Quinn ignored them all, and talked about the decorating they were going to do, and mending the fireplace to have log fires as soon as possible. Rebecca wondered how they could think of anything else but the serpent. She couldn't. Suppose she never saw it again. Suppose she never heard the haunting music again either. Her lunch seemed tasteless and impossible to swallow.

★ ★ ★

That night, Rebecca could not get to sleep. The silence seemed eerie. There was no music. Suddenly she heard a door creak, some footsteps and a slight rattle.

'The padlock chain,' she thought, jumping out of bed and pulling on her dressing-gown.

She found Rufus outside, trying to unlock the padlock of the ruined room, to her astonishment, then rage. For on the floor beside him was an unmistakable package.

'The serpent!' She tried not to shout, knowing
that the rest of the family was asleep. 'What have
you done with it?'

'I just hid it,' said Rufus defiantly. 'Because I
was cross with you. Being so horrible.'

'But you might have damaged it, you silly . . .'

'I haven't done anything to it and I'm putting it
back.'

'I've been so worried,' said Rebecca. 'How
could you steal it like that?'

Her voice rose and so did Rufus's.

'I didn't steal it. I hid it. In a very safe place.'

At that moment they both blinked as the landing light was switched on, and Mrs Quinn came out
of their bedroom, screwing up her eyes in the bright
light.

'What are you two doing? Isn't it enough to
have you sulking all day without disturbing us

having a shouting match in the night?'

'He took my serpent,' complained Rebecca, at the same time as Rufus was saying:

'I didn't do it any harm. It was a sort of joke.' But his words faded away as his mother glared at him.

'Not very funny. Neither is this quarrelling. You can both go straight back to bed. And I shall have the serpent in our room. Good-night.'

★ ★ ★

The next evening was the last rehearsal before the carolling on Christmas Eve. Rebecca and Rufus managed to avoid each other in the big house. She busied herself checking torch batteries with Peter, but it did not stop her hearing some careful practice going on in Rufus's room.

'At least he's hitting the drum, not you,' commented Peter. 'And now you can stop moping about the serpent.'

'I wasn't moping,' said Rebecca. 'It was a wicked thing to do. He might have broken it, past *ever* being repaired.'

'He's not that stupid. You just got on the wrong side of him when *he* was already worried he wasn't beating in time, so everyone might laugh at him on the big day.'

'They wouldn't,' said Rebecca quickly.

'Well, you seemed scornful enough to him. It's meant to be for fun, don't forget.'

'There's not much fun left at the moment,' said Rebecca sadly. 'Even with the serpent back.'

'Where is it now?'

'In their bedroom. Mum was so cross with us last night, I haven't dared to mention it yet.'

'I didn't hear you myself. Sleeping with a clear conscience, of course! But Dad was moaning. And I heard Mum say she'd like to bang your heads together. But he said leave you to fight it out.'

'I see,' Rebecca commented flatly.

Peter looked at her miserable face. Even the wisps of her tied-back, long hair looked lank. 'It is our first Christmas here in the village, you know, and Mum and Dad are making the house so nice. You two seem set to spoil it, though *you* have started something which might go on for years and years, it's such a good idea.'

'It was.'

'I think,' said Peter slowly, 'that you should bring out that serpent. Not hide it away. Clean it up as far as you can. Then let's have it out, hanging on the wall. Be proud of it for all of us, as it really started the band. Then, when you can pay to have it restored, *you* can learn to play it, perfect notes and all that to your heart's content.'

'I never could be a good serpentist,' Rebecca told him. 'It'll be far too hard to play.'

'But you know what I mean.'

'And if the haunting music stops?'

'That's a risk you'll have to take. I expect you'll go on hearing it, like people hear bells in their head. You're so . . .'

'It's easy for you to talk,' said Rebecca. 'Rufus has been a pest.'

'You were at his age, and you're fairly normal now,' said Peter. 'You're older than him, so I think it's up to you. Go and read some *words* of the carols. Forget the music for two minutes. I'm going out shopping with Dad now. Christmas secrets!'

Rebecca wandered up to her room, and rather resentfully began to look at the book of carols. She knew what Peter was telling her, but, cross though she was, she had to admit that the carol said it better.

Forgetting old wrongs with carols and songs,
To drive the cold winter away.

By teatime, Rebecca knew what to do. She found Rufus and said to him: 'I heard you practising. And it sounded fine.'

He looked surprised and muttered, 'I hope so.'

'You know what Mr Alexander says. It will be all right on the night. And we do have one more practice all together.'

'And,' said Rufus, swallowing hard, 'I could always ask you to hear me if I got anything wrong tonight.'

'Of course,' said Rebecca.

No more needed to be said. The battle was over.

8

A village band

At the rehearsal, Mr Alexander coaxed everyone to sing and play better than they had believed possible. 'You sound a bit like a band now,' he told them. 'Perhaps we should try out some more music in the new year, not disband!'

Rebecca was secretly proud of Rufus, watching Mr Alexander with such intent, knowing most of his music by heart now he had practised so much. All round her she felt a mounting excitement which had started as soon as they left Westy House. 'It's because of our first performance, I suppose, as well as Christmas. Perhaps I'll be nervous tomorrow,' she thought.

They arranged to meet at the church on Christmas Eve at six o'clock, with instruments, torches, music, 'and empty stomachs,' suggested Mr Alexander. 'I think we'll be made welcome in several homes.'

Walking up to the church from Westy House, the Quinns seemed to gather up people. Anne had called for them. Mr Button came out of his house as they passed. Two singers joined their group. Cottages with open curtains showed sparkling Christmas trees.

'I can't wait till tomorrow,' said Rufus. 'All the presents.'

'Tonight's lovely,' said Rebecca, feeling that nothing could match a meeting of so many new friends to make music together.

Mr Alexander wore a big duffle coat and gloves and was counting everyone as they arrived. 'We're all here,' he said. 'The sooner we start, the more money we collect. We'll sing a couple of carols under this lamp post, and Rose will go and knock on the doors and collect from everyone in this row of cottages, as they'll all hear us. We're collecting for the Save the Children fund. You've got the tin, Rose?'

'Yes, Mr Alexander.'

They had arranged that Rebecca would 'announce' each carol by playing the first line, so she had to know them by heart. The other players too could not read music and play. Only the singers could try and read the words they didn't know, and turn over pages with cold fingers.

Mr Alexander had not worried too much if people just sang the tune at their own pitch, rather than holding a part in alto, tenor or bass, and somehow the mixed voices blended and did not crack, as they had in the rehearsals.

When the collector signalled that she had been to all the cottages they moved on, glad to do so, as it was cold standing still, and Rebecca was par-

ticularly grateful for the fingerless gloves which kept her hands warm for holding the clarinet.

They walked briskly, to get warm, and someone murmured, 'Hurry' when Mr Alexander announced that the vicarage would be the first stop. The carols went well, although it was different singing in the open air, and the sounds seemed to evaporate a little.

'Keep quite close together, as long as you've room to play,' advised Mr Alexander.

Rebecca was relieved that it was not raining on her clarinet, and suddenly wished that she could carry the serpent proudly within the band. 'Perhaps one day that will be possible, and someone will manage to play it,' she thought. 'But the bass clarinet is a lovely sound. I'd like to try one of those next.'

At the vicarage they had coffee or squash and hot sausage rolls. At Evalina's they were given sweets and satsumas. Everyone seemed pleased to hear them, and several old people mentioned singing round the village when they were young.

'Yes, it does seem like Christmas Eve,' said Mr Button. 'I was doing up my presents all day to be ready for going out tonight. It's not often I venture out in the dark, but with the band and all these friends about me, I'm well away.'

He was glad sometimes to sit on a low wall for a carol or two as they gradually made their way

down the village. Rebecca wondered if Mr Parfitt
ever took his serpent out for Christmas carols and
sat on a wall to play.

Westy House was the last stop. Mrs Quinn had
stayed at home, and, as soon as the first notes
sounded, opened the front door wide and beckoned
them all inside. They squeezed into the back room,
where a big log fire was crackling and glowing.

'You can ask for what you wish,' Mr Alexander
said. 'We're not quite hoarse yet, nor worn out.'

'Then could I have the Somerset carol, please?'
asked Mrs Quinn, smiling at Rebecca. 'It seems a
special one to us this year.'

Rebecca felt that they had never played or sung
better, and wished they never had to stop. She
looked at the serpent hanging on the wall. Perhaps

Mr Parfitt brought his band to play in this room long ago.

When the carols ended she and Peter were busy helping Mrs Quinn pour drinks and hand round mince pies, cakes, crisps, biscuits and Christmas cake, for which somehow everybody found room, in spite of all they had eaten before. It was cosy after the cold night outside, and Rebecca was pleased to think she was at home. Then she realised just how much she felt at home in Mellford. As she sat listening to all the chatter round her, Mr Alexander stood up and said loudly:

'Before we find it's Christmas day and before we leave I must say thank you to all the Quinns for their kind hospitality. And most of all, thank you to Rebecca, who first thought of the Mellford band

and singers, who have sung so many carols tonight. One Christmas leads to another, but perhaps in between we'll be able to sing and play together again. I certainly hope so. I'm sure we have raised a lot of money in the heavy tin which has been handed to me.'

Everyone clapped, while Rebecca felt too shy to say anything, though they were all looking at her.

Matthew Quinn came to her rescue and said: 'I won't say it's been the quietest of terms here at Westy House, but it has been one of the happiest, and we have enjoyed most of all making so many new friends in Mellford.'

One by one singers and players said goodbye, then dressed up warmly to go out into the wintry darkness. Rufus admitted that he might be a little tired. Rebecca felt wide awake, with the carols still singing in her head. She said a private good-night to the serpent, whispering, 'Thank you, Mr Parfitt. I think I know now why your music has only played to me. And I did get your message. So I hope you liked the band. I promise we won't let it all fade away after Christmas. You've joined us to the village with your music.'

When she was in bed she lay waiting for the haunting music. At first nothing sounded. Then, as she drifted into sleep, the Somerset carol began. Rebecca smiled, even as she slept.